From Sea To Shining Sea

BY CALLISTA GINGRICH

ILLUSTRATED BY SUSAN ARCIERO

★ ★ ★ ★ ★ Acknowledgments ★ ★ ★ ★ ★

Thank you to the extraordinary group of dedicated people who made this book possible.

I especially want to thank Susan Arciero, whose superb illustrations have once again brought Ellis the Elephant to life.

The team at Regnery Kids has made writing *From Sea to Shining Sea* a real pleasure. Special thanks to Marji Ross, Cheryl Barnes, Diane Reeves, and Patricia Jackson for their insightful and creative contributions. Regnery has been remarkable in turning this book into a reality.

My sincere gratitude goes to our staff at Gingrich Productions, including Ross Worthington, Bess Kelly, Christina Maruna, Woody Hales, and John Hines. Their assistance has been invaluable.

Finally, I'd like to thank my husband, Newt. His enthusiasm for this series has been my source of inspiration.

Cataloging-in-Publication data on file with the Library of Congress
ISBN 978-1-62157-253-4

Published in the United States by
Regnery Kids
An imprint of Regnery Publishing
A Salem Communications Company
300 New Jersey Avenue NW
Washington, DC 20001
www.RegneryKids.com

Manufactured in the United States of America
10 9 8 7 6 5 4 3 2 1

Books are available in quantity for promotional or premium use.
For information on discounts and terms, please visit our website: www.Regnery.com

Distributed to the trade by
Perseus Distribution
250 West 57th Street
New York, NY 10107

To America's courageous pioneers who forged a growing nation.

★ ★ ★ ★ ★

Ellis the Elephant loved the American tale,
where courage, determination, and freedom prevail.
He wanted to know how America came to be
a nation united from sea to shining sea.

The country was young and needed to elect
a strong president the people would respect.
George Washington had led the American Revolution,
and became the first president under the Constitution.

Ellis read how the people searched for a place
to build a new capital the nation would embrace.
To honor a man who helped make America free,
they founded a city called Washington, D.C.

Congressmen and senators from each and every state
met at the Capitol for political debate.
Elected to serve and to make big choices,
they came to represent America's voices.

Ellis was surprised the president could command
whether Congress's bills became the law of the land.
The Constitution called for real cooperation
between these two branches to govern the nation.

President John Adams was second to preside,
but in Washington, D.C., the first to reside.
It was here that he lived with Abigail, his spouse,
in a home we know today as the White House.

Thomas Jefferson was elected president number three,
and was eager to grow the "land of the free."
He looked to the west for America to expand,
and signed a treaty with France for a large piece of land.

The Louisiana Purchase added much to explore,
in a nation now twice as big as before.
Ellis wondered why the French had agreed to the deal—
for half of a continent, the price was a steal!

The territory treaty now settled and signed,
Jefferson was curious to see what he could find.
He asked his friend Meriwether Lewis to start
a daring expedition to explore these new parts.

Lewis knew he needed all the help he could get.
The task was quite daunting, he had to admit.
So Lewis decided before he'd embark,
he wanted to bring his dear friend, William Clark.

Together, they assembled a talented team
to join them as part of this perilous scheme.
"The Corps of Discovery," as the group was known,
would venture together into the unknown.

In Illinois they gathered to train and prepare,
and strengthen themselves for the voyage they'd share.
Upriver they sailed into the western frontier,
on a journey that would last for more than two years.

Ellis was excited the adventure had begun.
Exploring the West seemed like so much fun!
But Ellis soon learned there was real work to do,
making maps, taking notes, studying specimens, too.

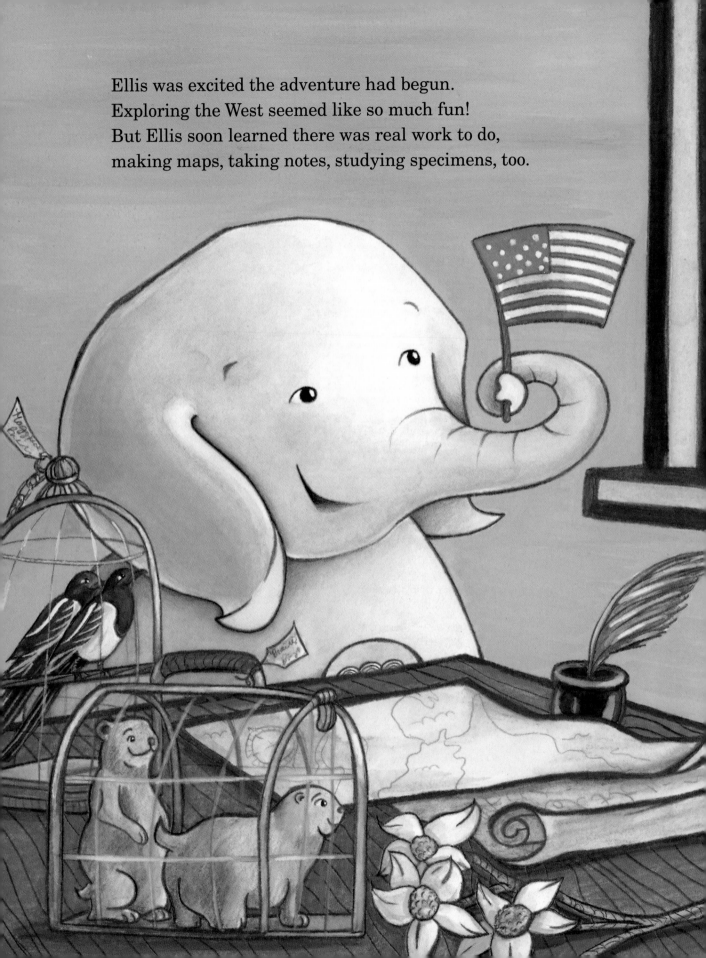

The journey continued as the weeks passed by,
and before very long, it was the Fourth of July.
To mark Independence Day for their young nation,
they fired a canon in great celebration!

The explorers made new friends nearly every day,
as natives guided Lewis and Clark on their way.
Soon they added a special friend to their crew.
Her name was Sacagawea, and she helped them get through.

She knew how to speak with the tribes and explain
their treacherous journey across the Great Plains.
Her husband came too as part of the team,
both earning the voyagers' love and esteem.

The North Dakota winter was terribly cold.
Waiting for spring, they put their journey on hold.
They selected a spot and constructed a fort
near a village of Mandans, who offered support.

The explorers liked the new tribe they'd befriended,
and spent time together as the long year ended.
Excited to see what the future would bring,
they gathered on New Year's to dance and to sing.

Along the way they encountered dangerous beasts,
including animals they'd never seen in the east.
One day Mr. Lewis had a terrible scare,
as he came face to face with a great grizzly bear!

The explorers had never seen grizzlies before,
and Ellis sure hoped they would not see more!
They took careful notes of the bear's every detail,
just like all discoveries they made on the trail.

For the rest of their journey they left horses behind,
since travel by river was now the best kind.
Their new friends, the Nez Perce, had tips they could use,
and taught the explorers to build dugout canoes.

The crew went to the forest and cut down pine trees,
then made sturdy boats with their friends' expertise.
To hollow the trunks they stoked fires inside,
and before Ellis knew it, they had a new ride!

The expedition moved west through difficult terrain,
steep mountains, rough rivers, and wide open plains.
Then one day the voyagers reached the Pacific.
Ellis was thrilled—exploring was terrific!

The travelers had gone as far as they could go,
blazing new trails for America to grow.
They stayed through the winter to enjoy what they'd found,
and when spring finally came, they were homeward bound!

Oregon
Country

British
Territory

Spanish
Territory

Louisiana
Purchase

Slowly brave settlers moved into the West,
forming new territories as they progressed.
Before long they petitioned to be states too,
admitted to the union, full of red, white, and blue.

Lewis and Clark Trail
Major stopping points

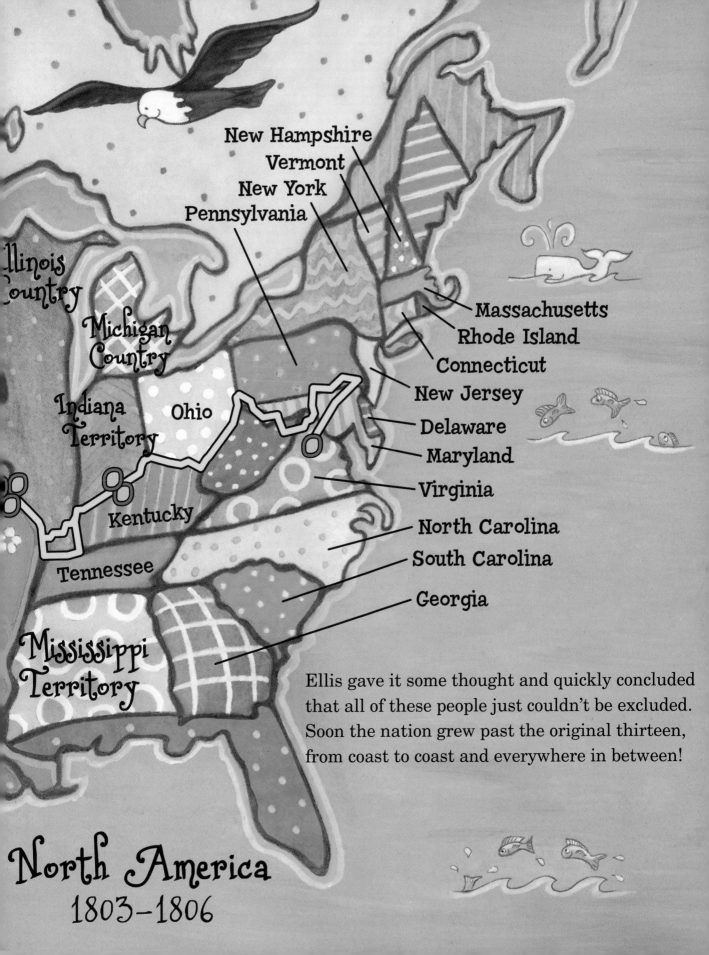

New Hampshire
Vermont
New York
Pennsylvania

Massachusetts
Rhode Island
Connecticut
New Jersey
Delaware
Maryland
Virginia
North Carolina
South Carolina
Georgia

Illinois Country

Michigan Country

Indiana Territory

Ohio

Kentucky

Tennessee

Mississippi Territory

Ellis gave it some thought and quickly concluded
that all of these people just couldn't be excluded.
Soon the nation grew past the original thirteen,
from coast to coast and everywhere in between!

North America
1803–1806

America had become such a large nation
that traveling through it took real innovation.
This was a challenge Robert Fulton understood.
He invented a steamboat and changed the country for good.

Ellis learned that steamboats quickly filled the rivers,
traveling north and south with cargo to deliver.
Ships were loaded with goods, passengers, and mail.
The Mississippi bustled when they all set sail!

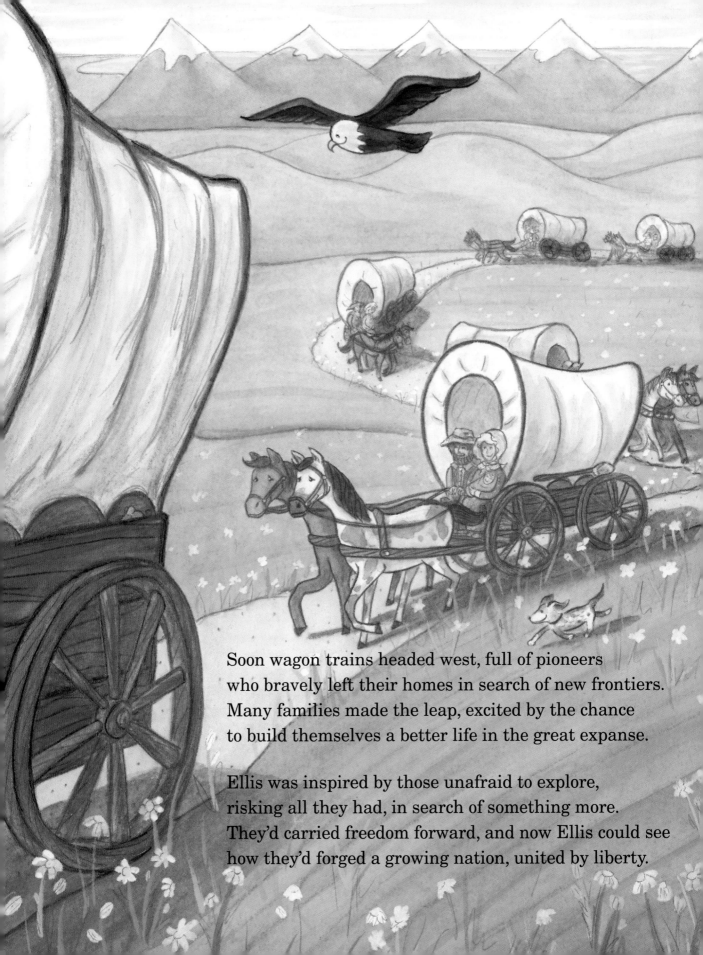

Soon wagon trains headed west, full of pioneers
who bravely left their homes in search of new frontiers.
Many families made the leap, excited by the chance
to build themselves a better life in the great expanse.

Ellis was inspired by those unafraid to explore,
risking all they had, in search of something more.
They'd carried freedom forward, and now Ellis could see
how they'd forged a growing nation, united by liberty.

★ ★ ★ ★ ★ Resources ★ ★ ★ ★ ★

Fun Places to Learn More about Westward Expansion

George Washington's Inauguration

On April 30, 1789, George Washington took the oath of office as the first president of the United States at Federal Hall in New York City, the nation's capital at the time. Washington had already devoted a lifetime of service to his country, most notably as commander-in-chief of the Continental Army during the American Revolution. As president, Washington set many important precedents, including the tradition of a peaceful transition of power after two four-year terms.

Explore George Washington's Life

Federal Hall ★ *Located on Wall Street in New York City, Federal Hall was home to the first Congress of the United States, and the place where George Washington was sworn into office as president.* ★ *Visit www.nps.gov/feha/index.htm for more information.*

Mount Vernon ★ *George Washington's home and estate in Mount Vernon, Virginia, is a national treasure, with a world-class museum and education center on the life of our first president.* ★ *Visit www.mountvernon.org for more information.*

Washington, D.C., and the Capitol

The United States Constitution created a representative legislature that was empowered to write and to pass new laws. Known as the Congress, the legislature consisted of two parts: the House of Representatives, in which states were awarded seats proportional to their populations, and the Senate, in which each state was represented equally with two seats. In 1790, the Congress created a national capital city in a new federal district called Columbia, situated on the Potomac River between Maryland and Virginia. The next year, the city was named Washington, after the country's first president. Construction on the Capitol building, where Congress would convene, began here in 1793.

Explore Washington, D.C.

Washington Monument ★ *Visit one of the most popular attractions in Washington, D.C., and get a bird's eye view of the nation's capital from the Washington Monument, a towering tribute to George Washington and the tallest building in the city.* ★ *Visit www.nps.gov/wamo/index.htm for more information.*

United States Capitol ★ *Visit the meeting place of the United States Congress to understand what makes representative democracy unique.* ★ *Visit www.visitthecapitol.gov for more information.*

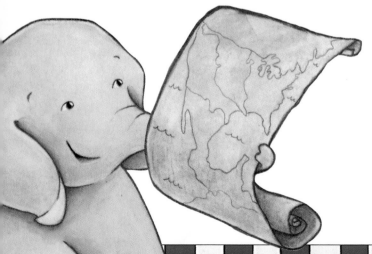

★ ★ ★ ★ ★ Resources ★ ★ ★ ★ ★

Fun Places to Learn More about Westward Expansion

The White House

In addition to the Congress, the Constitution created an executive branch of government headed by the president. The president was responsible for administering the country's laws, but he also had the power to veto, or reject, new legislation passed by Congress instead of signing it into law. This ensured that Congress and the president had to work together to govern the nation. Construction on the executive mansion began in 1792, and in 1800 President John Adams became the first chief executive to reside there with his family. The building was not officially known as the White House until 1901.

Explore the White House

The White House ★ *Enjoy a tour of the most famous home in America, while learning about the many changes that the White House has undergone since President John Adams first occupied the residence.* ★ *Visit www.whitehouse.gov/about/tours-and-events for more information.*

The Louisiana Purchase Transfer Ceremony

In the early years of the United States, Spain and then France claimed Louisiana and the territory west of the Mississippi River. At the beginning of the 19th century, the region became more difficult for France to maintain, and it negotiated to sell the land, including the important port city of New Orleans, to the U.S. In 1803, President Thomas Jefferson agreed to purchase this enormous territory, nearly doubling the size of the country for the bargain price of $15 million.

The treaty was signed in Paris on April 30, 1803, and the transfer ceremony took place the following December in New Orleans, Louisiana.

Explore the Louisiana Purchase

The Cabildo ★ *In New Orleans, explore the site where the Louisiana Purchase transfer ceremony took place in 1803. The Cabildo also served as the New Orleans City Hall until 1853.* ★ *Visit www.crt. state.la.us/louisiana-state-museum/museum-sites/ the-cabildo/index for more information.*

The Meeting of Jefferson and Lewis

Following the Louisiana Purchase in 1803, President Jefferson decided to send an expedition to explore the new territory and identify a water route across the continent. He turned to his personal aide, Meriwether Lewis, to head the expedition due to Lewis's experience as an Army captain and his knowledge of the western frontier. Lewis, knowing he would need help leading the expedition, asked his mentor from the Army, William Clark, to join him.

Explore Thomas Jefferson's Life

Monticello ★ *Discover the home that Thomas Jefferson began building in 1768 and continued to work on for more than forty years. Here you can see innovative architectural design, beautiful furnishings, and artifacts from the Lewis and Clark expedition.* ★ *Visit www.monticello.org for more information.*

★ ★ ★ ★ ★ Resources ★ ★ ★ ★ ★

Fun Places to Learn More about Westward Expansion

The Corps of Discovery

In the winter of 1803–1804, the Corps of Discovery (explorers who participated in the Lewis and Clark expedition) assembled at Camp Wood in modern-day Illinois to prepare for the long journey west. About thirty men spent the winter there on the Missouri River, along with William Clark who took charge of their training and packing. In May of 1804, Lewis and Clark and the Corps of Discovery embarked on their trip up the Missouri River in one large keelboat and two smaller vessels.

Explore the Corps of Discovery

The Lewis & Clark Boat House and Nature Center ★ *This museum dedicated to the Lewis and Clark expedition sits on the Missouri River in St. Charles, Missouri, not far from where the Corps of Discovery embarked on its journey.* ★ *Visit www.lewisandclarkcenter.org for more information.*

The Fourth of July

On July 4, 1804, one and a half months into their journey up the Missouri River, the explorers held the first ever Independence Day celebration west of the Mississippi at their camp in modern-day Kansas. They marked the occasion by firing their ship's cannon at sunset.

Explore Lewis and Clark's Fourth of July Celebration

Independence Creek-Lewis & Clark Historic Site ★ *The Corps of Discovery stopped at this small tributary on July 4, 1804, and named it in honor of the occasion. The site also features a reconstruction of a Kanza Indian home, since the explorers report in their journals that they spent the night near an abandoned Kanza village.* ★ *Visit www.travelks.com/listings/Independence-Creek-Lewis-Clark-Historic-Site/13157 for more information.*

Sacagawea

The Corps of Discovery made slow progress on the Missouri River throughout the summer and early autumn of 1804, and by October the expedition had reached current-day North Dakota. There, among the Hidatsa tribe, they met a French-Canadian trapper named Toussaint Charbonneau who lived in the village and was married to a young Shoshone woman believed to have been kidnapped and brought to live with the Hidatsa. Her name was Sacagawea. Lewis and Clark promptly hired Toussaint and Sacagawea as translators, and the couple joined the Corps going forward.

Explore Sacagawea's Homeland

Sacajawea Center ★ *This education center outside of Salmon, Idaho, is dedicated to preserving the legacy of Sacagawea.* ★ *Visit www.sacajaweacenter.org for more information.*

★ ★ ★ ★ ★ Resources ★ ★ ★ ★ ★

Fun Places to Learn More about Westward Expansion

Winter at Fort Mandan

Sacagawea and her husband joined the Corps of Discovery at Fort Mandan, where the group spent the winter of 1804–1805. The explorers developed good relations with the local Mandan villages and other nearby tribes. William Clark recounts in his journal how, on New Year's Day of 1805, sixteen of the men visited one of the villages to dance and play music at the request of the chiefs. Later that winter, Sacagawea gave birth to a son at Fort Mandan, whom she brought with her when the expedition continued later that spring.

Explore Fort Mandan

The North Dakota Lewis & Clark Interpretive Center ★ *Located in Washburn, North Dakota, this reconstruction of Lewis and Clark's Fort Mandan offers a glimpse of what life was like on their expedition.* ★ *Visit www.fortmandan.com for more information.*

The Explorers Encounter a Grizzly Bear

One of the most important aspects of the Lewis and Clark expedition was its scientific mission. Both men took careful notes on every aspect of their trip, describing hundreds of native plants and animals, as well as the people they encountered. Lewis and Clark sent dozens of specimens and artifacts back to President Jefferson to be studied more closely— including a few live animals. In April 1805 in current-day Montana, the expedition encountered and killed a grizzly bear. It was the first time the species had been described for science.

Explore Lewis and Clark's Scientific Mission

Academy of Natural Sciences ★ *Most of the specimens Lewis and Clark sent back from their journey were deposited at the Academy of Natural Sciences in Philadelphia, Pennsylvania, where the collection remains on display.* ★ *Visit www.ansp.org for more information.*

★ ★ ★ ★ ★ Resources ★ ★ ★ ★ ★

Fun Places to Learn More about Westward Expansion

Lewis and Clark Meet the Nez Perce

The expedition met the Nez Perce after crossing the Rocky Mountains near the borders of modern-day Idaho and Montana. The tribe welcomed the tired group with hospitality, offering food and advice about the journey ahead to the Pacific. Lewis and Clark decided during their stay to leave their horses with the Nez Perce and to continue with the remainder of the trip by river. Observing the explorers struggling to build new boats, the group's new friends taught them to hollow out canoes using controlled fires. Eight months later, on their return journey, Lewis and Clark met the Nez Perce again when stopping to pick up the horses they had left in the tribe's care.

Explore Lewis and Clark's Encounter with the Nez Perce

Nez Perce National Historical Park ★ *See where the Lewis and Clark expedition camped with the Nez Perce.* ★ *Visit www.nps.gov/nepe for more information.*

The Expedition Reaches the Pacific

On November 15, 1805, in what is now Washington state, the Corps of Discovery finally reached the Pacific Ocean. Since it was late in the year, the team resolved to stay on the west coast for the winter. Every member of the expedition, including Sacagawea and William Clark's slave, York, voted on the best site to construct their camp, which became known as Fort Clatsop. This would be the final winter of the expedition. In March 1806, they packed up and began the long journey home. They did not arrive back in St. Louis until the end of September 1806.

Explore Lewis and Clark's Pacific Coast

Cape Disappointment State Park ★ *Discover beautiful hiking trails and beaches and see where Lewis and Clark first saw the Pacific Ocean in 1805.* ★ *Visit www.parks.wa.gov/486/Cape-Disappointment for more information.*

Fort Clatsop ★ *Experience the camp where the Corps of Discovery spent the final winter of its journey.* ★ *Visit www.nps.gov/lewi/planyourvisit/fortclatsop.htm for more information.*

★ ★ ★ ★ ★ Resources ★ ★ ★ ★ ★

Fun Places to Learn More about Westward Expansion

A Growing Nation

The United States began growing almost as soon as it became a country. Many of the original thirteen colonies ceded their expansive western frontiers to the federal government in the years following the American Revolution, and from these, along with land acquired from British Canada and the Louisiana Purchase, the government formed several territories. The territories organized their own legislatures and once they reached a sufficient population, they petitioned for statehood. After the thirteen original colonies, Vermont, Kentucky, Tennessee, and Ohio were admitted to the union by the end of Jefferson's presidency in 1809.

Explore the Beginnings of Westward Expansion

The Museum of Westward Expansion ★ *Learn about the Americans who traveled west at the Gateway Arch in St. Louis, Missouri, the city where many pioneers began their journey.* ★ *Visit www. gatewayarch.com/experience/the-gateway-arch/ museum-of-westward-expansion for more information.*

Advent of the Steamboat

The inventor Robert Fulton designed the world's first commercially viable steamboat, the *Clermont*, which embarked on its first trip up the Hudson River from New York to Albany in August 1807. Before long, steamboats became a vital mode of transportation throughout the United States. The Mississippi River got its first steamboat, the *New Orleans* (another Fulton ship), in 1811, and within two decades the river was host to hundreds of others. This innovation proved invaluable to the commercial and territorial expansion of the United States.

Explore the History of the Steamboat

The Hudson River Maritime Museum ★ *Learn about the* Clermont, *Robert Fulton's first steamboat in Kingston, New York.* ★ *Visit www.hrmm.org for more information.*

The Mississippi River Museum at Mud Island ★ *Learn about the history of the Mississippi River and board replica steamboats in Memphis, Tennessee.* ★ *Visit www.mudisland.com for more information.*

★ ★ ★ ★ ★ Resources ★ ★ ★ ★ ★

Fun Places to Learn More about Westward Expansion

Pioneers Head West

In the decades following the Louisiana Purchase, millions of Americans moved west to start new lives for themselves and their families in territories stretching all the way to the Pacific Ocean. Many settlers traveled in caravans called wagon trains, most famously on the Oregon Trail over a route similar to the one Lewis and Clark had pioneered. America's expansion did not come without costs, however. With each new territory, Americans confronted the contentious question of whether slavery would be allowed. Moreover, as settlers migrated west they displaced many native people who were there before they arrived. Eventually, relations between the settlers and the Native Americans deteriorated to the point that the U.S. government relocated many tribes into designated areas known as reservations. Our country still struggles with the consequences of these actions today. There is no doubt, however, that the courage of the early pioneers eventually helped extend the freedoms guaranteed in our Constitution to everyone from coast to coast.

Explore the Legacy of Westward Expansion

The National Frontier Trails Museum ★ *Learn about the Oregon, Santa Fe, and California Trails, which originated in Independence, Missouri. ★ Visit www.ci.independence.mo.us/NFTM for more information.*

National Museum of the American Indian ★ *Learn about the history of Native Americans at this inspiring museum on the National Mall in Washington, D.C. ★ Visit www.nmai.si.edu/home for more information.*